To my sweety
Shoshi with lots of loves!

Francesca

This edition published by Parragon in 2013
Parragon
Queen Street House
4 Queen Street
Bath BA1 1HE, UK
www.parragon.com

Adapted by Xanna Eve Chown
Based on the original teleplay by Teri Weiss
Illustrated by Artful Doodlers

ISBN 978-1-4723-0673-9
Printed in China

nickelodeon

DORA the EXPLORER

Dora's Dance Show

Bath • New York • Singapore • Hong Kong • Cologne • Delhi
Melbourne • Amsterdam • Johannesburg • Auckland • Shenzhen

¡Hola! I'm Dora and this is my best friend, Boots. I love to dance! Today is a special day for my dance class. We're putting on a show for our friends and families. We just need one thing before we start – our dance slippers!

Look! It's the Delivery Duck with a delivery from the Dance School. Wait! These aren't dance slippers, they're scuba flippers! We can't dance in these

¡No se preocupen! Don't worry! I'll go back to the Dance School to find our dance slippers. Map will know the way. Help me call him. Shout "Map"! Shout louder – "MAP"!

Map has found the quickest way to the Dance School. We have to go past Bunny Hop Hill and through Benny's Barn. *¡Vámonos!* Let's go! We can dance along the way.

¡Baila, baila, baila! Dance, dance, dance! Did you know that dancing is a great way to make you feel happy? You can't feel sad when you're dancing!

Look, there's Tico! He's sad because his balloon has popped. Dancing will help Tico to feel happier.

Oh no! Isa is sad because she dropped her ice cream cone. I know how to cheer her up. Dance with us, Isa, and you'll soon be smiling again!

We made it to Bunny Hop Hill and cheered up our friends along the way! But now we need to find a way through these three doors. *¡Hola, conejito!* Can you help us? The bunny *says* we just have to play Follow the Bunny. Will you play too? Great!

Let's hop like a bunny to open the first door. **HOP, HOP!**

Shake your bunny tail to open door number two! **SHAKE** with me!

The last door will open if we wiggle our bunny ears. **WIGGLE, WIGGLE!**

Good job! We made it through Bunny Hop Hill to Benny's Barn. Benny says we've arrived in time for the Animal Dance Hoe-down. Listen to him sing!

"We're at the Animal Hoe-down!
There's no time to slow down!
Because at the Animal Hoe-down,
Got to dance like the animals do!"

Benny says we should dance like the animals. First try to HOP like a frog, then GALLOP like a horse and finally ... FLAP like a chicken! Hey, you really know how to move!

Now we need to find the Dance School! Which path should we take to get there – left or right? *¿La izquierda o la derecha?*

Yes! It's the one on the right. Let's go!

Oh no! The school gate is locked. How are we going to get in? We'll need a key. Look, there are five keys on that branch. And they're dancing a conga!

Wait! Did you hear something? It sounds like Swiper the fox. He wants to swipe the keys! Quick, help us stop him. We've got to say, "Swiper, no swiping!" Say it with us,

"Swiper,
NO
swiping!"

Hooray! We stopped Swiper. The keys are so happy they are doing a dance. Be careful keys! You're at the end of the branch....
"Conga, conga, conga!"

Oh no! The keys are falling and they're heading for that puddle. There's only one thing to do - a big, dance leap!

One, two, three....

Leap!

Look, the lock has four points. So, the key that fits will have four points too! Which key is the right one? This one has one, two, three, four points. It fits!

We're inside the Dance School. But where are the dance slippers?
Which box do we need?
There it is! *¡Fantástico!*

¡Rápido! We need to get back to the Dance Show with the slippers as quickly as possible. Everyone is waiting for us. I know what will help us get back really, really fast ... the Dance Train!

We have to sing the Chugga Chugga Choo song to get the train moving. Come on, join in!

¡Gracias! Thank you, Train! That was very fast. Hey everyone, we're back, and we've brought the dance slippers. Quickly, let's put them on. Now we can start our show.

Wow! It's so exciting to be dancing on the stage.
The audience is clapping and I can hear Mami and Papi cheering.
¡Gracias, gracias¡
Thank you, everyone!
We did it!

We really enjoyed trying out all those different dances today. Boots liked it best when we flapped like chickens in Benny's Barn! What was your favourite dance? That was my favourite too! Thank you for helping. See you soon!

The end